222

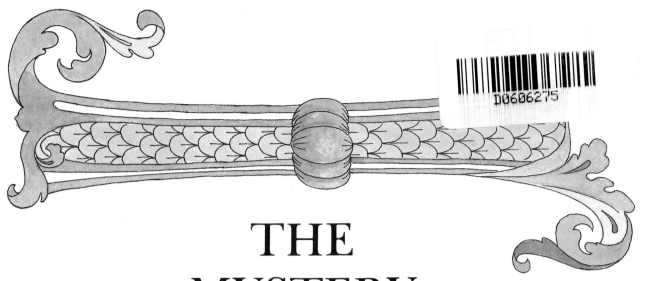

THE MYSTERY
of the
FLYING MONK

Text by Antonio Tarzia
Illustrations by Gino Gavioli
Translated by Edmund C. Lane, S.S.P.

ALBA · HOUSE alba house NEW · YORK

SOCIETY OF ST. PAUL, 2187 VICTORY BLVD., STATEN ISLAND, NEW YORK 10314

JOHN THE BAPTIST ELEMENTARY
LIBRARY MEDIA CENTER

alba house

© Edizioni Paoline s.r.l., Cinisello Balsamo (Italy)

© Copyright 1990 by the Society of St. Paul
ISBN 0-8189-0583-2
Printed: 1990

One fine day, while getting water from the fountain just outside the city gate, Grandma Matilda began to shout: "I see him! I see him myself! Look, he's right there in the basin!"

I rushed to get a look and in my hurry lost my balance. I fell into the fountain and got myself dripping wet.

I even might have drowned had it not been for a brawny robust shepherd who at that moment was passing by. Used to handling sheep, he drew me out of the fountain in one fell swoop.

As I was drying my clothes before the open hearth, Grandma Matilda finally began recounting her vision to me: "And don't you tell me, too, that it was just the reflection of a passing cloud, because I know very well what I saw and I cannot be wrong! It was Brother Giles, that saintly man, who flies about the heavens like a bird. I saw him. I saw him as clearly as I see you. He was wearing his brown habit with the cincture and was mirrored in the water with the archangel Gabriel."

I listened with my eyes wide open, between one sneeze and the other, and so wished that I had seen him too. Everyone was talking about this holy friar who flew so high into the heavens that he became as tiny as a swallow, but no one knew where he lived or where he came from. When I grow up, I told myself, I'll become a monk and fly freely over the woods and above the houses, too.

On the feast of Saint Ubaldo, bishop of Gubbio, while I was rummaging through the fruit stands and the stalls where geese and baby pigs were sold, I had the good fortune to run into a friar begging alms. He was standing in front of a little stage laughing as he watched an acrobat perform. He kept on chuckling even when I asked him about Brother Giles, the flying monk. He didn't know him, he said. He didn't belong to his monastery on the coast. "Maybe he's from a monastery up north. Try looking for him there."

After the fair, the whole town fell silent. The monotony of every day returned. There was nothing new to do. Every day it was the same old thing. The traveling merchants, the jugglers, the flute and mandolin players had taken with them the joy and color of the feast.

I was overwhelmed by a feeling of sadness and by an ever more burning desire to fly. I spent my days watching the swallows and their complicated patterns of flight as they filled the heavens with their shrill cries. Almost without knowing it and without my having decided to do so, I found myself far from home in the countryside, stealing fruit and begging bread: "If I could just dress up like a monk," I told myself, "then maybe I could fly." And I kept on walking, walking, walking.

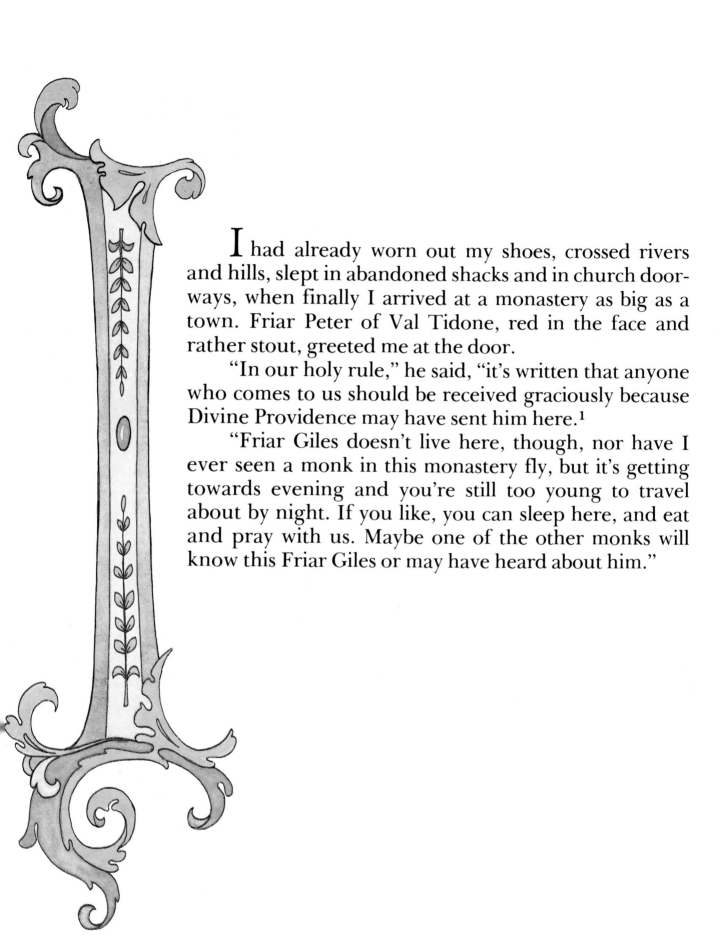

I had already worn out my shoes, crossed rivers and hills, slept in abandoned shacks and in church doorways, when finally I arrived at a monastery as big as a town. Friar Peter of Val Tidone, red in the face and rather stout, greeted me at the door.

"In our holy rule," he said, "it's written that anyone who comes to us should be received graciously because Divine Providence may have sent him here.[1]

"Friar Giles doesn't live here, though, nor have I ever seen a monk in this monastery fly, but it's getting towards evening and you're still too young to travel about by night. If you like, you can sleep here, and eat and pray with us. Maybe one of the other monks will know this Friar Giles or may have heard about him."

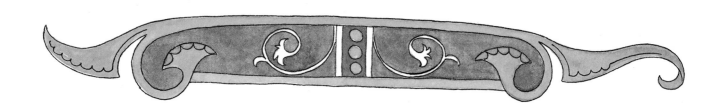

I couldn't refuse such an inviting offer. Then, too, I was very hungry and afraid to go about at night when all the shadows are so hard to make out and sounds and voices acquire such strange and mysterious echoes.

I had seen the monks one day reentering the monastery down by the seashore after a liturgical procession. It was the monastery to which the begging friar belonged. The monks were walking single file like a line of ants. And after the last one entered, the door slammed shut with a resounding thump, thus separating and isolating the monastery from the rest of the world. At that time, I tried to imagine what might be going on inside that "anthill," but I had no clear idea.

The monastery of Friar Peter was very well laid out, with covered walkways enclosing courtyards with fountains and flocks of snow white doves. On one of the walls there was a sketch of the whole complex with the church, the buildings, the courtyards and the garden. An inscription beneath the sketch read: "The Celestial Jerusalem."

Watching the "anthill" was a lot of fun, like wandering around the county fair. Everyone was doing something: some were tending the flowers, others were chasing after the chickens, while still others were fixing the roof. Only the oldest were sitting around reading or praying and for these there was always a ray of sunshine which reached them where they were to warm them up a bit.

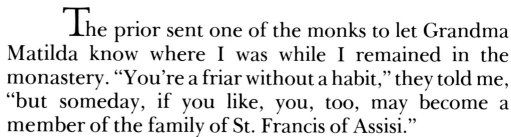

The prior sent one of the monks to let Grandma Matilda know where I was while I remained in the monastery. "You're a friar without a habit," they told me, "but someday, if you like, you, too, may become a member of the family of St. Francis of Assisi."

It would have pleased me no end to be a monk. They were all so happy. They never fought with one another or insulted one another. And when they encountered each other in the walkway or in the garden, they always wished each other "Peace and all good things."

At the same time, my longing to fly was still very strong. From Friar Centenary (everyone called him that, for he was very old and had a long white beard) I learned that Friar Giles, when he was learning how to fly, used to go up into the bell tower. So quietly, quietly one day I climbed up to the top of the bell tower and there encountered a curious surprise.

Friar Gino from Milan liked to bring tomatoes up there to dry in the sun and, without the others knowing, he would color the eggs of the pigeons and the doves: "That way," he said, "for them it is always Easter and it makes them happier."

But the most likeable and jovial monk in all the monastery was Friar Checco from Sedilo. When he was a boy he went to war and fought against the Saracens with an enormous sword which he kept hidden in the wine cellar.

The wine cellar, chock-full of vats, barrels, bottles, urns and jars of wine was his kingdom. Even when he was distilling the wine to make grappa he would pray, and stay there whole days at a time without going out into the fresh air.

One day he told me, "Come and I'll let you sip something fit for a baby's tongue. It's not much more than colored water, but it has such a nice taste and aroma."

G. GAVIOLI-

One night I heard the bell calling the monks to prayer and got up out of curiosity. The friars were leaving their cells not altogether fully dressed, but already chanting the psalms and, according to Franciscan conventual tradition, trying to conquer their sleep by singing praises to the Lord.[2] Only one of them seemed to have no trouble keeping awake: Friar Mentolo who at that hour was slipping in by the garden gate with his basket full of night herbs.

When the moon was full, Friar Mentolo (who also had the proper name of Agilulfo and who was originally from the Valley of Brembana) would go out into the fields and woods to collect his medicinal herbs: "Washed in the light of the moon," he used to say, "they become more beneficial."

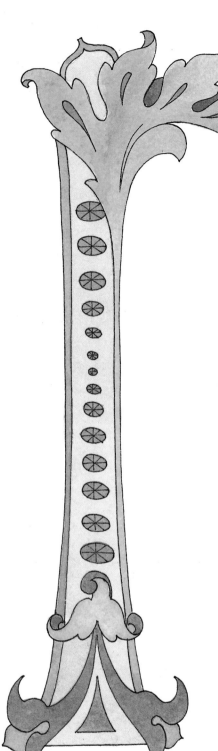

The notes of the organ, played with gusto by Friar Paul Bitetto, put everyone in a happy mood and the song of the monks rose majestically to the ceiling inviting the sun, the moon and the stars to likewise praise the Lord.[3]

They sang like men in love, with the exception of Friar Centenary, who wandered around the monastery all day reciting prayers and now, during Matins, got up "because the Bible said to"[4]; but, once in church, made himself comfortable and dreamt of the angels. "The angels are all masters of song," he used to say, "and so true is this that they are divided into choirs and are often pictured playing instruments."[5]

Not even when it rained or snowed did life in the monastery come to a halt. There was so much to do in the garden, in the stables and around the house that no one could give in to laziness. And then the teaching of Francis was always very much alive: "I wish that all my brothers would work and give themselves humbly to honest labor so as to be of little burden to the people, and that their hearts and tongues not give in to sloth. If one doesn't have a skill of some kind, let him learn one."[6]

Friar Mentolo handled his roots and herbs with the extreme care of the druggist, but with a whole lot more love. The herbs were for him like little children that had to be taken care of and nurtured, following even their little whims: "Some, for example, are poisonous, but others become so only when they are badly handled."

He knew the time for each plant's ripening and how it should be harvested; from some he plucked only the flower, from others he took the stem, and from still others he collected the tuber or the bulb.

"The cane and the gentian are good for the digestion," he would say, "the horse chestnut is good for the skin."

"If a wasp stings you, apply a slice of onion and if you suffer from kidney stones use cinnamon."

"Remember that dog's grass detoxifies the liver, aloe is good for cuts and burns, while horseradish lessens the pain of sciatica."

"If you suffer from loss of appetite, try a bit of wild chicory." The concoctions, infusions, teas, and medicinal eye drops that Friar Mentolo prepared had an almost miraculous healing power, so much so that many came from far away to buy their pharmaceuticals.

G. GAVIOLI -

Friar Gino from Milan was a painter, a master of color and design. He had turquoise eyes and red hair, and looked much younger than he was. "Everyone who comes to my studio," he complained, "admires my icons, my sketches, and my miniatures and then asks: 'And the artist, where is he?'"

"Of what use is it to be good at painting, to have a sense of color, and know how to put gold leaf on miniatures, if you don't have a white beard and everyone takes you for an errand boy?"

That was the great pain of Friar Gino, the miniaturist who, every year on the Feast of the Epiphany, would dress up like one of the three kings, with a crown on his head and a long white beard made of lamb's wool. The gift which he brought to the prior was always the same: a miniature book finely hand drawn. Over the years he had illustrated *The Little Flowers of St. Francis*, the biography of St. Francis of Assisi written by Tommaso of Celano, the *Lauds* of Jacopone da Todi and the *Legend of Saint Clare*.[7]

Every once in awhile you would see Friar Mestolo, armed with a long knife, running behind a crowing cock who had shown him no respect and whom he had condemned to the grill, without however ever succeeding in his intent. The cock had no intention of being martyred like St. Lawrence and so there followed flights and rapid chases around the garden, through the kitchen and at times even up into the bell tower.

Friar Mestolo (that was what everyone called him even though he was really named after the prophet Samuel) was an exceptional chef who was able — using ordinary garden vegetables, a couple of sauces and three aromatic herbs — to put together a princely feast, fit for a cardinal from Rome.

His soups and sauces — of almonds, leeks, beans, grated lettuce, and zucchini — were as good at telling the time of the year as any calendar: whether it was February or April or May or July. If potato soup were served you knew it was September; in October, mushrooms; in November, cabbage; and from under the December snows, you could expect a sauce made from apples and dried prunes.

"A good cook," he used to say, "can do without meat or fish, but not without eggs and milk; if you want to take the pleasure out of eating, do away with the milk and eggs."

With the aid of these two ingredients and a fist full of flour, Friar Mestolo could put together the sweetest smelling and most appetizing desserts made with carrots, egg plant, lemon, chestnuts, or dog-rose berries.

One especially hot day, the friars swarmed out of the monastery for the harvest. They went to help the countryfolk gather in the wheat, as Francis and his first companions did.[8] The farmers, in exchange for this help in the fields, generously provided the monks with flour for their bread and straw for their beds.[9]

I was told to stay at the monastery to keep Friar Centenary company, and so I passed the time talking with him about Friar Giles who, he told me, was very devoted to his Guardian Angel. In fact, he had a picture of his Guardian Angel in his cell, and whenever he went up into the bell tower to fly, he always had his Guardian Angel with him.

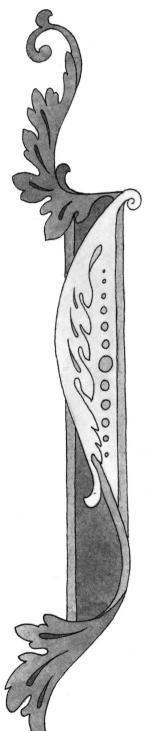

In the days following the harvest there was fresh bread for all without needing to beg for it. Friar Mestolo cleaned the old stove, then busied himself about it all day working up a sweat, finally bringing to the table the most beautiful and delicious smelling rolls imaginable. It was bread made with the flour which was donated and hence blessed: and for this reason it was customary to kiss it before eating it and to praise the Lord before enjoying it.[10] I hid a piece and took it to a stray dog who had become my friend and who was always waiting for me just outside the monastery door.

Eating it with him, I recited the prayer which the friars said: "If you share your bread with the hungry . . . then your light will break forth like the dawn . . . justice will go before you . . . and if you call upon the Lord, he will respond."[11]

On October 4th, the Cardinal Protector of the Franciscan Order paid a visit to the monastery. He arrived with all his retinue because he was making a long trip: "I'm happy for the opportunity to stop in this oasis of peace," he said, "and to celebrate with you the birth in heaven of St. Francis of Assisi."[12]

Then, in his lengthy homily during the Mass, he said that Francis, before he died, had given to his Friars a piece of memorial bread, recalling what Jesus had done at the Last Supper.[13]

Friar Mestolo was preoccupied, because he didn't have any more of his good fresh bread and was afraid of making a bad impression on a person of such high rank; also because it was traditional in the Order to treat the Cardinal Protector with special esteem.[14]

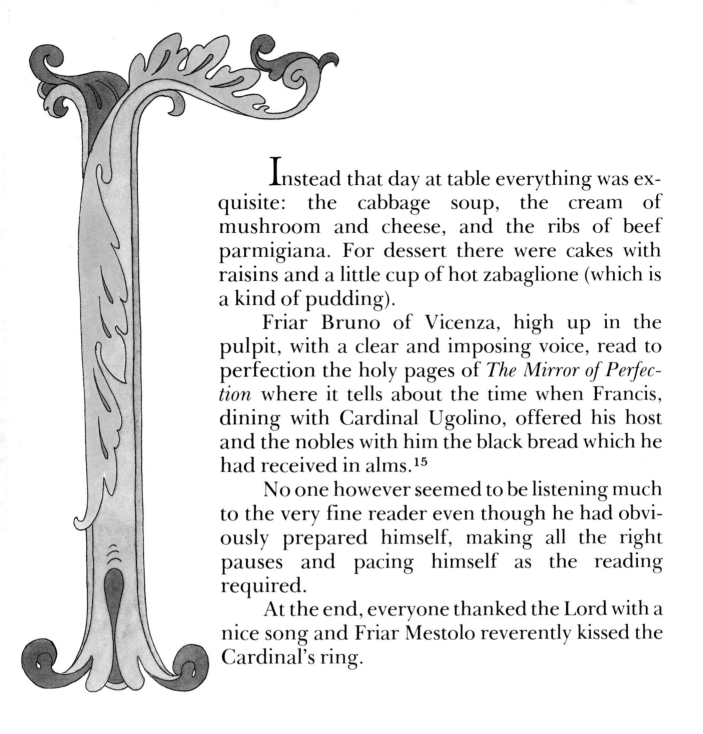

Instead that day at table everything was exquisite: the cabbage soup, the cream of mushroom and cheese, and the ribs of beef parmigiana. For dessert there were cakes with raisins and a little cup of hot zabaglione (which is a kind of pudding).

Friar Bruno of Vicenza, high up in the pulpit, with a clear and imposing voice, read to perfection the holy pages of *The Mirror of Perfection* where it tells about the time when Francis, dining with Cardinal Ugolino, offered his host and the nobles with him the black bread which he had received in alms.[15]

No one however seemed to be listening much to the very fine reader even though he had obviously prepared himself, making all the right pauses and pacing himself as the reading required.

At the end, everyone thanked the Lord with a nice song and Friar Mestolo reverently kissed the Cardinal's ring.

Up to this time I had never managed to enter the library, a place for reflection, study and learning. Friar Marino from Mondovi, the librarian, had told me that not even the novices were permitted to rummage through the old books where the knowledge of good and evil could be found. I was just a youngster still.

But, given my insistence, one day he let me in just beyond the door and showed me a great big book where the story of Friar Giles — "the monk who knew how to fly like a kite and to soar like the royal seagull till he was swallowed up in heaven's blue" — was told and illustrated.

I read the whole story more than once, so that I learned it all by heart. "If he was able to make himself so light and free as to be able to fly like a bird," I told myself, "then I'll succeed in doing so too, once I am big."

Then they took me home. Grandma Matilda was very proud of me and asked me to tell everyone the marvelous tale of Friar Giles. I hope to go back to that monastery one day. Who knows? Maybe I could learn to fly, too, like the mysterious Friar Giles. Or become a saint like Francis, who caused the earth to bloom wherever his foot trod, so caught up was he in the beauty of the stars, of "Brother Sun" and "Sister Moon."

NOTES

1. *Regola non bollata*, 11:1.
2. *Leggenda dei tre compagni*, 11:41. Bonaventure of Bagnoregio, *Leggenda maggiore* 8, 10: "During his stay up there, a falcon who had its nest in that spot, attached itself to Francis in a bond of unwavering friendship. During the night, it would anticipate with the sound of its song, the hour when Francis was used to getting up to recite the Divine Office. That pleased the Servant of God very much, because the great effort which the falcon made to be up and doing in turn encouraged him to throw off any feeling of slothfulness or lethargy."
3. Psalm 148:3.
4. Psalm 119:62.
5. It was Pseudo Dionysius the Areopagite who organized the hierarchy of angels into nine choirs: seraphim, cherubim, thrones, dominations, virtues, powers, principalities, archangels and angels.
6. *Specchio di perfezione*, 75.
7. *La leggenda di santa Chiara vergine* was penned around 1255-56 at the request of Pope Alexander IV by a Friar Minor who remains anonymous. In it the life of Saint Clare is narrated from the time of her birth to her canonization.
8. *Leggenda perugina*, 10: "Fairly often, in order not to be without anything to do, they would go out to help the poor people in the fields, receiving at times some bread offered to them for the love of God."
9. *Specchio di perfezione*, 5: "So great was their poverty that their cot or bed, if they had a rag they could throw over the straw, would be considered a nuptial couch."
10. Francis did this at table with Cardinal Ugolino, Bishop of Ostia: Tommaso da Celano, *Vita seconda*, 73.
11. Isaiah 58:7-9.
12. Francis died on the evening of October 3, lying on the bare earth. The next day, which was a Sunday, his body was taken from the Porziuncola to Assisi and buried in the church of San Giorgio.
13. Tommaso da Celano, *Vita seconda*, 217.
14. *Regola bollata* XII, 4: "Moreover, out of obedience, he ordered the ministers to ask the Pope for one of the cardinals of the Holy Roman Church, who would be the governor, protector and corrector of this community." Francis personally asked Pope Honorius that Cardinal Ugolino, the Bishop of Ostia, might be made the Protector of the Order. Cf. Tommaso da Celano, *Vita seconda*, 25.
15. The *Specchio di perfezione* or *Memorie di frate Leone* is a collection of facts and legends about the life of St. Francis of Assisi which dates back to 1318.

Printed: 1990 from type set in the U.S.A.
Istituto Grafico Bertello - Borgo San Dalmazzo (CN)
Italy

JOHN THE BAPTIST ELEMENTARY
LIBRARY MEDIA CENTER